Phoenix Young Readers' Library

Captured by Raiders

Phoenix Young Readers' Library

1.	Lots of Wonders	Sam Mbure
2.	The Sun and the Wind	Anne Matindi
3.	The Pet Snake	Dickson Mukunyi
4.	The Greedy Host	J.K. Njoroge
5.	The Speck of Gold	Cynthia Hunter
6.	The Peacock and the Snake	Elijah K. Soi
7.	Cock and Lion	Kalondu Kyendo
8.	Beautiful Nyakio	Frederick Ndungu
9.	Children of the Forest	Joel Makumi
10.	Mzee Nyachote	Roeland Japuojo
11.	The Fly Whisk	Stephen Gichuru
12.	The Talking Devil	Leo Odera Omolo
13.	The Feather in the Lake	Joel Makumi
14.	Give the Devil his Due	W.K.Boruett
15.	Inspector Rajabu Investigates	F.Kawegere
16.	The Powerful Magician	Daniel Irungu
17.	End of the Beginning	Joel Makumi
18.	Onyango's Triumph	Leo Odera Omolo
19.	Tales of Wamugumu	Peter N. Kuguru
20.	The Girl who Couldn't Keep a Secret	Clare Omanga
21.	Wake Up and Open Your Eyes	Edward Muhire
22.	The Proud Ostrich	J.K. Njoroge
23.	Njogu The Prophet	Jamlick Mutua
24.	Travels of a Raindrop	David Ng'osos
25.	The Adventures of Thiga	C. M. Mureithi
26.	Pamela the Probation Officer	Cynthia Hunter
27.	Anna the Air Hostess	Cynthia Hunter
28.	The Circle of Revenge	David Mwaurah
29.	Town Tricksters	David Mwaurah
30.	Truphena Student Nurse	Cynthia Hunter
31.	Truphena City Nurse	Cynthia Hunter
32.	The River Without Frogs	Writers' Committee
33.	The Great Siege of Fort Jesus	Valerie Cuthbert

and more.... many more

Captured by Raiders

BENJAMIN S. WEGESA

PHOENIX PUBLISHERS, NAIROBI

First published in 1969
This edition published in 1989 by
Phoenix Publishers Ltd.,
Grain Belt Industrial Park,
Sukari Industrial Estate,
Off Thika Rd., Behind Clay Works,
P.O. Box 30474 - 00100,
Nairobi, Kenya.

© Text: Benjamin S. Wegesa, 1969,1989
© Illustrations: Phoenix Publishers Ltd.

ISBN 9966 47 099 9

Reprinted in 1991, 1993, 1995, 1996, 1997, 1998, 2000, 2001, 2002, 2004, 2005, 2006, 2008, 2009, 2010, 2011, 2012, 2013, 2015, 2016, 2017, 2019, 2021

Printed by
Modern Lithographic (K) Limited,
P.O. Box 52810 - 00200,
Nairobi, Kenya.

Contents

1. The Tondo spy 1
2. The attack 10
3. The long journey 17
4. Life in a Tondo family 25
5. A dangerous escape 33
6. The farewell 48
7. Encounter with a snake 55
8. The fatal fall 62
9. A fight with a lion 72
10. Home at last 77

TO ESTELLE HOLLINSHEAD: with whom I spent many hours at Lugulu Girls' School trying to open up the way for the Nanjalas and the Nekoyes of Africa, this book is affectionately dedicated.

1

The Tondo spy

The sun was sinking slowly down the sky, spreading its warm rays over the lonely Sawenja hills. Most of the herdboys had driven their animals across the hills and were now in the Sirisia Valley leading them home. The mountain birds were singing their sweet lulling-songs to the tired sun, the warbler, the sun-bird, the owl and even the dove taking part in filling the evening air with music. Our animals were moving in a single file down the hill, with my brother, Kakai, in the lead lazily playing a home-coming tune on his *mulele* flute. I was at the rear end of the file, a small girl of about eight, greatly interested in looking after our animals like the other children in the Sawenja hills. I walked impatiently behind the last beast trying to make him walk faster. The air was cool and peaceful and the hyraxes, squirrels and mountain rats playfully jumped in our way and then darted behind the rock shelters as we tried to hit them.

While I was trying to chase a squirrel which had come very close to me, I suddenly saw a man armed like a warrior, complete with spear, sword and shield sitting behind a rock, his red eyes gazing widely at the disappearing animals. His sandalled feet were restlessly tapping the ground as though impatient to

be on the move. Although I cried out in fear when I saw him, he did not change his position to look at me, but silently and motionlessly watched the marching animals.

Sensing the danger that we all faced, I fled from him, feeling with every step I took that his spear was being thrust through my flesh. Over rocks, in and out of bushes, across flowing streams of water I ran, as fast as my feeble feet could carry me. When my brother Kakai saw me racing along, he followed without making any attempt to ask what had happened, and, as though summoned by the spirit of the dead, the animals came running after us. When we got home, we found mother in the kitchen finishing her cooking. I took her by the shoulders, and shaking her violently, told her about the man. "He just sat there, Mother, behind the rock like a dead man, except that his feet were moving."

"What do you say? Was the man dead?" she asked, throwing down her ladle.

"Who was he?" she questioned, faking my shaking hand.

"A man, Mother, a Lang'o," I muttered, through my quivering lips.

"Oh stop, child!" my mother ordered. "I know you are wrong. Our men are everywhere on the boundaries keeping very careful watch. Your grandmother has talked so much about these Lang'o that you seem to see them behind every bush." Then, looking at my brother, she asked, "Did you see him, Kakai?"

"No, Mother, I ran only because she ran. I did not see anything, and I don't think there was anyone."

I opened my mouth to argue with them, to prove to them in some way that I had seen the man, but mother held her finger up to stop me from saying anything more. I went outside and wept bitter tears of frustration because neither of them believed that I had made an important discovery.

When evening came, I wanted to mention the afternoon's experience to my father, but I was afraid that mother would not let me repeat it, so I kept quiet and ate a hasty meal with my parents before going to my grandmother's house to sleep. If only I had known that this was to be the last time that I would live in that home, I would have stayed and talked longer. How I wish I had realized that it was nearly the last time that I should see my father alive! I would have stayed longer.

When I told the story to my grandmother, she listened to me with great understanding and asked me many questions about the man: his clothes, his weapons, his hair style, his looks and even the colour of the clay he had on his face. She nodded her head at every answer as if remembering something.

When I had finished talking, she looked up at me and said, "You're a sensible girl, Nanjala. This man was not a Lang'o, he was a man from the North. We call his tribe the Tondo. They are the fiercest people in the North and have defeated all the other tribes. We have not fought against them for a long time.

When I was a girl about your age, they attacked our village and drove us out of the land of Bubulo, behind the great mountain of Masaba. They killed half of our people and took all the animals. My brother, Nato, and your uncle, Bakasa, were killed during the fight. The rest of us escaped and walked for many days, carrying nothing from our homes. After long days of travel, we managed to cross the great Masaba mountain, and settled in this place. We did not hear of the Tondo again for many years, but a few months ago when I was coming from Namawanga, I unexpectedly ran into a friend of mine from the North. She told me that the Tondo had crossed the mountains and were raiding homes and taking away animals, children and women, and putting to death everyone who resisted them. She said that they had captured many villages, and were settling on this side of the mountain. That was several months ago, but the Tondo are never in a hurry when they prepare to raid. They plan wisely and usually send their spies ahead of time to find out the living conditions, the type of country, the kind of animals, the watch kept by the villagers and the easiest way to get out of the land after a raid. From what you have told me, I am convinced that these terrible people are here again."

After a long silence, my grandmother stood up and said, "I must see your father about this. I am sure that he will take action when he fully understands that our tribe is in deadly danger once more." Before I could say another word, she had flung open the door and disappeared in the darkness.

I sat there before a dying coal of fire, shaking like a frightened chameleon on a feeble twig, partly from the cold wind and partly from the fear of the invading Tondo tribesmen. Terror caused my feet to shake so violently that I could not even walk to the door to shut it. Time went by, and with its passing, courage failed me completely, leaving nothing in my whole being except violent, overwhelming fear. Once or twice I decided to plunge into the dark night and follow my grandmother, but stopped myself for fear that I might find myself caught in the Tondos' trap.

I sat there for a long time waiting and hoping for grandmother's return. Kakai, who also shared grandmother's hut, did not come either. "What's happening?" I asked myself out loud. With the question still on my lips, I stood up and shut the door.

I had almost given up hope for my grandmother and my brother, feeling that they must have been killed by the Tondo, when the door opened and both of them entered. Grandmother sat down in the doorway quietly puffing at her smoking pipe. Kakai came and sat beside me at the fire-place as I anxiously waited for one of them to break the silence. Peering through the darkness of the hut, we could distinguish our grandmother's body doubled up in the doorway, her eyes gazing away into the darkness. Once in a while she would shake her head regretfully as though answering our childish questions, and then she would mutter something between her closed lips, in the way she spoke when talking to the spirits of the dead. After what seemed an eternity to me, she shut the door, walked to her bedroll, dropped down like a log of wood and slept. Realizing that she had no intention of telling me what father had said, I made my bed and lay down to rest.

I closed my eyes and tried to force myself to sleep, but still I saw the Tondo behind the rock. I struggled to fathom what it all meant and opened my eyes, but they could not penetrate the darkness. As the agonizing moments dragged by, fear possessed me so much that I could not contain myself any longer.

"Grandmother," I whispered, "What did Father say?"

"Your father does not understand, Nanjala. Like all men in this country, he no longer capes what may happen." She kept quiet for some time, then added, "He blames me for it. He says that I made you see the man." Then she was silent for so long that I thought she had fallen asleep, but presently she whispered, "Nanjala, are you still awake?"

"Yes," I answered, afraid to say any more.

"The Tondo will come. It may not be to-night. It may not be tomorrow, but they will come one day. I want you to know how to escape when they do come. They never attack during the day. No, not the Tondo. They always attack during the night. They choose a dark night like to-night when the sky is covered with clouds. They send three or four people to lie in wait at pre-arranged places, then at a given signal they make a concerted attack.

"When this takes place there will be great commotion and shouting amongst our own villagers. When you hear this noise do not go out of the house. If you do, you will be killed. Wait until the fighting has been going on for a short while, during which time men from other villages will rush in to support our men. They will come with noisy yells and cries, and a great battle will follow. While this is in progress, the Tondo will make every effort to get away with the cattle. This will be the time for you to seek safety outside the house. If you stay inside longer than this, you will be burned alive. The Tondo never leave a village until they have burned down the last house. Go out by the back door and climb up the nearest tree. You ought to be safe, but if they catch you, do not resist, just go with them. One day you may find a way to escape.

"This country needs you, Nanjala," she continued dreamily. "We cannot afford to lose you at your age. I am ready to die because I have lived long enough. I have produced men who have fought in famous battles and achieved greatness. I have produced women who have served great warriors; but the time for fighting with swords and spears and considering cattle-wealth as the greatest glory is gone. The time when women sit at home taking care of the young ones and waiting for orders from their men folk is almost past. You are on the threshold of a new era when women will work and fight side by side with men. You will live in a world where women will eat chicken, and will even become leaders of their own people. You will live through the days of the palemen, who will come following a black string which they will lay down from the great sea of Walule to the great sea of Sisumo. You will live under a new order and among new people.

"The palemen will take away your cattle and will give you broad beans which you will value more than cattle. They will turn your warriors into cooks. As I cooked for your grandfather, so will they cook for the palemen. Their women will be honoured more than the warriors of our land are honoured today.

"The palemen will grow wings and will fly above your heads like birds, and will move as fast as lightning. Their arrows will roar like thunder and will kill by sound alone. Yes, the palemen will have all the power and you will no longer fear the Tondo or the Lang'o or the Sebo. This is the last attack you will ever face from the Tondo. If you are not killed, lead your people. Fight for the women of this country to enable them to throw off the burden that they have carried all these years. You have the wisdom to lead others. You have the eyes to see, use them. You have the ears to hear, listen to greater voices." She lay down again and that was the last time I heard her reassuring voice. I lay there quietly thinking about the seemingly impossible things that my grandmother had said. After a long while I fell asleep.

2

The attack

I had been sleeping for probably two hours when I was awakened by the mournful sounds of warning drums. Tibuu! Tibuu! Tibuu! The sound filled the stillness of the night. My grandmother stirred, but said nothing. Kakai sat up and said, "Grandmother, do you hear that?" She did not answer, so I went over to her intending to shake her out of sleep but she was not sleeping; she was wide awake, calmly puffing at her unlighted pipe. While the two of us moved restlessly from one corner of the hut to another, the war-horn sounded the signal, its long sharp blast striking the rocks in the hills and coming back to us in blood-chilling echoes.

"We must run away and hide," my brother said, shaking with fear.

At this remark Grandmother jumped up, and grasped each of us by the hand. We pulled and shouted in fear, wanting to escape, but like a carpenter's clamp, her grip held us tighter and tighter. War had begun, and already the groans of dying people filled the air. Here a cry, and there a shout for help. From one house came the mooing of cows, from another the bleating of sheep, and from yet another the screaming of terrified children, and everywhere the sound of running feet;

but familiar noises assured us that the men from the other villages were coming to our aid. The moments that followed were of such great confusion that we did not know who or what would be left alive after the battle. When the centre of confusion moved a little to the north of the village, our grandmother suddenly released us from her strong grasp, opened the door and mercilessly pushed both of us out, then shut the door behind us. I could not understand such cruel treatment and tried to force the door open, but she had bolted it on the inside. Kakai, like an escaping gazelle, darted away to the bush. I stood outside the hut in a dazed state before a great desire to find out what had happened to my parents took possession of me. I squeezed my fingers and bit my tongue in childish rage, wondering whether I should risk going home alone, or climb a tree as I had been advised.

I do not know what force carried me, but before I knew what I was doing I found myself in our house, looking for my parents, feeling empowered to protect them. There was no sound in the house. All the animals had been taken away. The door, having been torn from its hinges, was lying on the floor. "Mother," I whispered in that insipid stillness of the dark night. "Mother!" I called again as if ordering her to life in case she was dead. There was no answer. In mounting frenzy, I searched impossible places: in every corner, behind every basket and under every grinding stone, leaving nothing unturned, there was no sign of my parents. I ran out and pulled some thatch from the roof of the house and lit a torch to find out exactly what had taken place inside. Thus satisfied, I began to take thought for my own safety. During the careful inspection of my home, I had worried for the safety of my parents and had completely forgotten the dangers that hung over my own head. All the horrors that had threatened me had faded away. In my mind there had remained only one thing, an urge to find and help my parents.

Suddenly I could hear, louder than ever before, screamings, groanings and wailings coming closer to the house. Throwing down my torch, I made for the nearest tree and like a scared monkey flung myself up it in a split second. There, hiding myself under the swaying leaves, I cried as I had never cried before. Then, I do not know what power possessed me, but somehow, I pushed myself into the fork of the tree and quickly fell asleep.

When I opened my eyes, a new day was beginning to dawn. Birds were singing in the trees and the eastern light was stretching its pale rays to the mountain top. There was smoke everywhere and the air was filled with the smell of burning animal fat. Painful groans of suffering people came to me from two or three places. I pushed aside the branches which were in my way, and there before me, I saw what I had feared to see — dead bodies in useless heaps. I tried to free myself in order to drop down and die, but the fork which had secured me for the night still imprisoned me. Just as I was trying to disentangle myself from the branches, I heard the cry of a running man screaming in fear. "Help! Help!" he cried. The voice was familiar; it came clear and plain through the air. Without a doubt it was my father's. I pushed the branches aside and looked. There I saw him, my own father, as tall as ever, running as fast as his apparent weariness would allow; and behind him two warriors chasing after him at a faster speed than he was able to make, their blood-bathed spears held high above their heads, their buffalo-hide shields clutched firmly under their arms and their clay-matted hair, like leopard's tails, swinging behind them. "Help! Help me! Someone help me!" Father shouted as he drew nearer to our home. The men were catching up with him, someone had to help him immediately or else he would be a dead man in a few minutes. I tried to shout to him, to call him to the tree where I was hiding, but my voice dried up in my throat and was never heard. I bit my fingers and twisted uneasily in the tree, and watching intently was amazed to see my father turn and make for the tree. He looked very tired and was giving up. "Father!" I shouted, anxious to give him new hope and courage. "Father dear! Run! Get up here!" I urged him on and he leaped to life and made big strides ahead of the overtaking warriors. Then it happened, exactly as I had feared: in trying to jump over a low bush father caught his foot in it and fell down immediately under the tree. I tried to close my eyes from the awful sight, but could, not. Father sat up and looked at me up there in the tree, his soft kind eyes appealing for help, his body drained of strength from hours of fighting. The warriors arrived and stood there, laughing at the helpless man.

"Take me prisoner," he pleaded. "Take me with you. I'll be your slave." But they only laughed and made faces at him. He pleaded again and begged them not to kill him. Then they started their song of victory, and danced round their prisoner while he held his head between his knees in an attitude of complete surrender. I closed my eyes against the worst, but they were not in a hurry to do anything. I even began to hope that they would take him prisoner, but while I was comforting myself with this hope, that which I had first feared took place: without, giving him time to say anything more, the warriors ended their dance with a game which froze the blood in my veins. They raised their bloody spears together and brought them down through my father's body. "Stop!" I shouted hopelessly from the tree. Father uttered a painful cry and fell down. Without thinking about my own safety, I jumped down from the tree to try and rescue him, but it was too late; he was dying. I knelt beside him and held his hand. Blood gushed from his side. "Father, don't, please don't die. I need you." He opened his eyes and looked at me. "Nanjala," he murmured, smiling at me in his usual loving manner, "you are a brave girl. Don't give up." He squeezed my hand and closed his eyes never to open them again. I knelt down for a long time holding his cooling hand, not knowing whether to cry or laugh, and hoping for a miracle that would bring him back to life, but I knew that all was over. He was dead.

Then I remembered the two Tondo warriors who had done this. "It is foolish of me to sit here while the people who have killed my father are standing there," I thought bitterly. "I must do something." I jumped up and faced the warriors. "You have killed my father," I shouted at them. "You will pay for it." I flew at one of them, biting his hands, kicking his feet, and tearing at him with my human claws in a fit of mad fury. He only laughed and seemed to take no notice of my childish attacks. Then, turning to his friend, he asked for a leather strap which was wound around his waist, and before I could resist him he pinned my arms against my body and began to bind me up in a neat bundle. Then he threw me down beside my father.

For a long time I straggled and twisted, and tried to bite at the strap while the men sat and talked endlessly.

I knew that they were discussing me, possibly wondering what they should do with me. I wished that I could understand the Tondo language in which they spoke, because then I could have given them some suggestions about what to do with me. They seemed to disagree with each other. The older man, who looked at me from time to time, seemed to think that I should be treated with favour. Once or twice he pointed to my father's body with his spear and then pointed it at me. The younger man shook his head and talked excitedly, evidently trying to convince the older man. They both stood up and examined my father's body. They looked at his feet and his hands and examined his teeth. They discussed each of these parts. Then they turned and examined me. They looked at my feet, my face and hair, each time comparing me with the dead body of my father. Convinced that there was some relationship, they agreed upon what to do with me. They spread out a leather sheet and I was rolled up in it like a dead animal and carried between the two men. When I looked up, I could see nothing but the sky.

3

The long journey

Thoughts raced through my mind as I was swung from side to side by the walking men: "Is my mother alive?" I asked myself. "Shall I ever be able to see my grandmother again?" I kept thinking as we went.

Over the hills, down the valleys we journeyed, never stopping for anything. The whole army of Tondo warriors enjoyed themselves in every respect as they drove the great herd of animals before them, now singing, now shouting with joy, now running or walking, but paying very little heed to me.

From the sound of mooing and bellowing, grunting and bleating I gathered that many different animals had been taken. We had been walking for many hours without a stop when I was carelessly thrown down like a bundle of wood. An old man uncovered me and untied the straps that bound me. He pulled me up to a standing position, but I fell back because my feet were unable to support me. "I am Kiprono," he said by way of introduction, addressing me in Lubukusu which many Tondo had learned from their prisoners. "Now that your father is dead, I will be your father." I wanted to jump at him and kick him, but my grandmother's last words sounded again in my ears, "Nanjala, if you are captured, do not resist. Just go with them. You may find a way to escape." I sat up straight and put on a false smile.

"What happened to my mother?" I asked him, keeping my voice steady.

"I regret to tell you that you are perhaps the only person from your village who has survived. As far as I know, everybody else was killed. We had captured a large group of women and children when your father and others attacked us and killed many of our men. In the battle that followed it appeared that we would be defeated and therefore we killed all our prisoners; but luck came to our aid and we won the battle. Your father was the last man to die. He was a brave man and killed many of our people. I would have killed you, too, but my own son was killed in the battle and I needed someone in his place to take care of my animals."

He stopped and looked at me with tears rolling down his face. "Your father killed my only son. I long for revenge. I wish I could kill someone whom he loved. I wish I could kill you, but you are only a woman, a frog, a helpless creature! Your father's spirit would laugh at me and make fun of me!" He lifted me up and held me tightly to himself as he shook with anger. I thought he was going to break my ribs. Then he let go of me and I fell down in a heap on the ground.

"Your father killed my only son," he moaned.

"Your son, your son!" I shouted in hatred from my huddled position. "My father killed your son! He ought to have killed you, too. He ought to have Killed the whole lot of you in the same way as you Killed all our people. Why did you leave me alive, you beast?" I jumped to my feet and flung myself at him. "Kill me now. What have you spared my life for? What is there in life for me now that you have killed all the others from my village? What shall I achieve in life? Shall I ever bring in a dowry to my people? Shall I ever bear men to fight for the Bukusu against their enemies? Shall I ever rejoice with my tribesmen in their victories at war? What shall I be? Tell me, what shall I be? Kill me!"

He looked at me with an expression as hard as granite and said, "If I kill you, my son will laugh at me. You are a woman. You cannot pay for his life. He was our best warrior. He was a warrior such as we shall never see again. You cannot pay for his life," he repeated.

We rested there for an hour or two. They milked the cows and drank the milk. They gave me a bowlful of it. Then they drained blood from the bulls and had a good meal.

When we left this first camp, they let me walk. My feet were still numb from the pressure of the straps that had bound me, but by degrees they became normal again. After three or four miles, the men noticed that it was not possible for me to keep pace with them. Two or three attempts to make me walk faster failed, so Kiprono picked me up and set me on the back of one of the cows. At first, I was afraid the cow would throw me down. She ran and kicked, hitting me with her tail. I lay flat on her back and held myself firmly by fastening my arms around her neck. After some time, she calmed down and began to walk gently. Kiprono walked close to me and said, "You are a brave girl. You equal my son in that respect." He put his hand on the back of the cow and walked silently by my side.

We had two or three other stops during the day to allow the animals to graze and rest, but no one talked to me at all.

They all seemed to be interested in talking about something that took their minds completely away from me. This gave me time to think about my loving parents and my brother Kakai. "Is Kakai dead too?" I asked myself, biting my tongue.

For several days we travelled over the mountains, through the forests, over the moorland and across the plains, having only periodic rests. Then I knew we were drawing near to our destination because the warriors began to blow their horns and dance. Presently we were joined by more and more people as we neared their homes. Men, women and children took part in the singing. Some shouted joyfully and laughed, but others screamed and wept as they mingled with the crowd. Then, from a nearby village, came a great crowd of women to welcome us home. Young women and old women, teenagers and junior girls, all came running to welcome us. First, they ran very fast. Then they slowed down as they drew closer, taking time to stop and dance with glee when they saw the big herd of cattle approaching; but the expressions on their faces changed after they had scrutinized the small number of warriors and realized how few were returning home, and as they fell into step with them their joyful singing gave place to mournful wailing. Mothers who failed to see their sons, wives who did not see their husbands, sisters who did not see their brothers, all shared in the sorrows of the day. During the confusion, I slipped off the cow that had so faithfully carried me for several days, and followed behind Kiprono. He walked quietly with his head bowed low, dragging his shield and spear behind him as a sign of grief and loss.

It was at this point that I realized how much Kiprono's son, who had been killed by my father, was loved by the villagers. They ran up to us, read the signs of grief that Kiprono displayed, and sped away to spread the news. When the whole mob learned of this great loss its joyful songs of victory turned into a mournful dirge. People gathered around Kiprono and escorted him towards his home, sorrowfully wailing and screaming. Kiprono held me by the hand as we continued our journey homewards. In misery and bewilderment, I walked by his side, not knowing what lay in store for me. Kiprono said nothing about his son's death. I had feared that the telling of his story would be the end of me; but it had still to be told.

As a lamb being led to the slaughter, I went forward, more pulled along than led by my will. When we reached the centre of the village everyone stopped. Kiprono lifted up his spear and the hundreds of voices that had mourned in unison were stilled.

At the time I could not understand what was being said, though I was well aware of the tense atmosphere and the response of the crowd to Kiprono's words. It was only later, when I had learned their language, that my foster-mother was able to give me the following account of what had passed that day and how my life had been saved.

"We have had a good battle," said Kiprono, in forced determination to control his emotion. "We have brought back a lot of animals, but we have lost many of our people. The Bukusu have learned to fight. They have killed the best of our men." He stopped. There was a long silence when nobody moved. Then his wife came forward and asked, "Did Kiptalel leave any word? Did you see him before he died?"

"No, Kiptalel did not leave any message. He died before I could reach him; but I killed this child's father, so I have brought her home in place of Kiptalel. I do not know her name yet, but I will call her Chesebe." He stopped and looked at me with tears in his eyes. "Her father killed my son." I almost fainted. At this juncture his wife caught hold of my hand. She was shaking with great anger.

"He did?" she asked, tightening her grasp.

"Kill her!" the mob shouted. "Give her to us if you cannot kill her." They pressed around me and for a moment I thought I would not see the sun again.

"Stop!" Kiprono ordered. "You are all cowards. You remained here when we went to fight. You are just like women. You would never want to go out on a battlefield and kill a man. You let old men go to bring animals and fall in battle; but when you see a girl, a child with her hands tied, you want to kill her. What has she done? Is she not just a woman without a soul? Is she not just a child, a woman without sweet blood? Step back!" he barked, and pushed them back. "Don't you know that I save father killing my son? So mercilessly killing my son, and yet for days I have held her hand to bring her here. I see no good in killing such a child. If you think her life has the same value as that of my son, then here she is, kill her! If you believe that her life would pay for the lives of more than fifty of the best warriors in this land who have fallen before the swords of the Bukusu tribesmen, then kill her! If you feel this will be enough revenge for what has happened to us, then cut off her head!" He pushed me into the middle of the crowd and shouted, "There she is! Kill her! Kill her now! You cowards, kill her! You men who lost your brothers, kill her! You women who have lost your husbands, kill the child! You mothers who have lost your sons, here she is, kill her!"

He pulled a sword from his belt and threw it towards them. "Here is a sword. Kill the child!" They all moved back with tears rolling down their cheeks. Standing there in their presence, I felt like a warrior myself. I could see sadness and defeat in their faces. Kiprono picked up his sword and walked away.

In despair, I followed his wife to her home yearning in misery for my own parents, for Grandmother and

Kakai, refusing to accept the fact that they were no longer alive. I glanced at our animals which Father had loved and spoken to in the way he would talk to people. I recalled how cruelly some of them had been treated by the Tondo when the poor creatures were too tired to move fast. As my mental agony increased, my anger mounted and I longed for power to defeat the hated Tondo and to drive our animals back home; but I was only a helpless young girl being led into captivity. If only mother had listened to me — if only she had warned our warriors, these terrible things might not have happened. I hurried forward and said to the woman, "Mother, kill me. If you kill me, you will feel better."

She stopped and smiled at me very sadly and answered in my language, "Why should I kill you? Kiptalel would despise me if I killed you." She shook her head and walked at my side almost proudly.

4

Life in a Tondo family

The houses in which the Tondo lived were very different from the homes of the Bukusu. Their houses were long, low-roofed barracks on the side of the mountain where three or four families lived together, separated only by low skin walls. Between each family compartment there was a big room where their animals slept. It was the breath of these animals that kept the rooms warm during the night. The furnishing in the houses was simple. In most of the family compartments there were one or two stools for the men to sit on. Several milk gourds, and half-gourds for drinking from cluttered one side of the firewood rack, while skin bed-rolls and wooden pillows were stacked on the other side of it. Earthen water pots were placed near the entrance, as were the men's spears, shields and clubs. Their food was simple. They drank milk and blood and ate semi-raw meat. For some months I found it difficult to live as they lived.

Mutua, my foster-mother, loved me very much. In all our talks she never mentioned her son. She asked me about my family and learned their names. She was very sorry when I told her how my father had been killed. "Oh deal', I am sure it was too much I for you to see all that," she said, "but then all brave I men should die in battle. It is only women who should die at home." These words comforted me a little.

We always worked together. We collected firewood, fetched water and picked fruits from the forest while the men hunted. In the evenings she told me stories about her tribe. Stories of battles' and of raids. Once in a while she would tell me stories about marriage. She was a good story-teller and always left me longing to hear more. "Tell me another, mother." I would beg her. "Chesebe," she would say, laughing, "tomorrow will come, too. You will need a story then."

One day mother came to me in a confidential way and said that I was now one of them, that I had learned their language quickly and seemed to enjoy their food, and was even thinking like a Tondo, so she had planned to have my appearance altered. "We must make you look like one of us," she confided warmly, "You need earrings in your ears to increase your beauty. You also need our tribal markings. These will make you attractive."

I protested strongly, "I have enough beauty — I need nothing to add to it!"

"Chesebe," she replied coaxingly, "you need to become a Tondo in every respect."

Day after day this matter was discussed and every time I showed angry displeasure; but Mutua was determined that I should be transformed into a Tondo girl. When the time came, my ear lobes were pierced open and ugly heavy rings fixed in them. My beautiful face was tattooed with many ugly marks, my teeth were cut according to their fashion, and even the lower lip of my mouth was pierced and a smooth round stone fitted into the opening to keep it open. It was a very painful procedure which took several months.

Every day I was taught the behaviour of a good Tondo girl. I spoke their language, ate their food and sang their songs. Men and women who visited the home liked me very much. They thought that I was one of the most beautiful girls they had ever seen. At least, they said so. I was hard working, and that made my foster-mother love me the more. I knew how to do my work without being told. I ran for water, fetched firewood, and collected fruits for the family.

One day, when I was clearing up in the house, I found some maize and bean seeds mixed up in an old basket. I asked mother to let me use them. "How?" she said. "Men brought them from a distant country and said that the people of the place did not eat meat. They eat these for their food. You can throw them away, if you wish. I do not care for, them." I thanked her and took away the seeds.

Working with a stick hoe in that rocky place was difficult, but eventually I opened a big enough garden to put in the seeds. Children from the village came and helped me clear it and they even did some digging. They also collected manure from the nearby cow-dung heaps. We spread the manure in the way my father used to do, and then planted the seeds. These turned out to be good, for they germinated well, and soon the children were coming to help me weed the garden. After a while I had a good crop of beans and some maize, though this did not do so well. It was at this time that I began to teach the women how to cook beans and meal-mash. At first they did not like this kind of food but by degrees they developed a taste for it. Many people came to taste it. Some liked it, but others did not care for it.

These periods of introducing my captors to my own people's ways of life gave me so much satisfaction that my hatred was not so fierce, but I still harboured bitter feelings against them when I thought of my family; and my yearning to return to my own country became almost unbearable. I became increasingly moody, and I would sit alone picturing myself making an escape.

As the days went by, I began to suspect that something mysterious was taking place. Many meetings were being held at our home which I was not allowed to attend. At first, I thought these were plans for more raids, until I remembered that mother had told me that they never drank *endali* (the wild fruit beer) at their raid-planning meetings, but at these meetings they drank a lot of it. When I asked her what the meetings were about, she only hugged me and laughed.

One day, while I was working in my small garden, trying to make it bigger for the coming season, I learned the truth of the matter and wished I had not lived to see that day. Chesang, my friend from the neighbouring village, had heard people talking about it and wanted to hear the facts from me.

"When do you go, Chesebe?" she asked, fixing her eyes on something in the woods. "Go where?" I questioned.

"To the big home. To your husband," she laughed.

"What do you mean? Husband?" I asked, becoming cross with her.

"Haven't you heard, Chesebe? Haven't they told you? The Chief needs a new wife. He has more than twenty wives, but must marry a new one each year. The women of the village choose the best girl in the location for him. This year, they have chosen you. I wish I could have this chance; he is a rich man and his women do nothing. They have servants to work for them and they have plenty to eat. You are lucky, Chesebe."

"Lucky!" I said. "I am only a child. I don't want to marry an old man. I want to grow up and marry a young man of my choice."

"Surely you don't mean it, do you?" Chesang looked at me wondering what stupidity I was talking. In her own tribe it was a great honour to marry a chief. She told me how it had taken these women a long time to make the decision and how they had been criticized for choosing a stranger. She said that I was the first stranger in all the lives of her people to be named for a Chief. She added that after long periods of observation, most of the elders agreed to accept the women's choice.

Her words pierced my heart like sharp spikes in the flesh. Each sentence made my heart ache with pain. I threw down my hoe and walked home.

My foster-mother was not at home when I got there. This suited me well. I walked to my sleeping corner, made my bed and lay down. My head was feeling dizzy, my eyes were heavy with tears, my hands were shaking with fear. It was quite clear to me that I would have to marry a Tondo one day, but this was not the man, and this was not the time.

As I lay there thinking, the idea of escaping presented itself more forcefully, but it was dismissed as being too dangerous, because I knew that the Tondo boundaries were very carefully guarded at all hours of the day and night. A successful escape would be almost impossible. I had heard of prisoners who had tried to escape and had been hanged for it. Furthermore, my foster parents were so good to me that I did not like the idea of leaving them and yet I was determined not to be forced to marry the Tondo Chief.

I must have lain there for hours, torn between two worlds, now my heart urging me to escape, now refusing the idea because of the sorrow it would bring to my foster-parents; now crying bitterly about this plan of marriage, now laughing at the idea of a child like me winning a great chief like Arap Koech. "It is your good luck, Nanjala," I told myself. "You will make a good wife for the great chief. He will love you and make you his favourite wife." Thoughts like these fed my pride and dimmed my vision of escaping, but in the end, I dismissed them as foolish. Then a thought flashed into my mind. I remembered Chepteek, a very nice, middle-aged woman who lived alone on the edge of the river Kaptumo. She and I had collected firewood in the forest on many occassions. I had helped her to gather roots for her supper when her supply of meat failed. I had even carried firewood to her home. On one occasion she had minted at being able to help me escape if the time ever came for me to try. She had helped other girls to make safe escapes, and wondered if I should like to try. I had told her then that I did not wish to run away from my foster-parents because they were so good to me; but it was different now. They were planning to marry me to an old chief with twenty wives. I had to do something to stop them.

When Mother came home sometime later, I was still lying there deep in thought. "Chesebe," she said gently, sitting down beside me. "You are sick, my clear!" I smiled at her lazily.

"No, Mother, not really sick but just resting after a long day's work. Is there anything I can do to help you, mother?"

"Much," she said, running her fingers gently through my hair. "Why not go to the forest and bring some firewood? I am going out for a drink so cannot go with you, but we need wood for tomorrow. We shall have a big day, dear, just for you," she added, laughing. She fixed her gaze upon my swollen eyes and said, "My child, you have been crying. What is the matter? Do you still think of your father and mother?"

I uttered a forced laugh and lied. "Oh Mother, they are long forgotten. The dead have a world of their own and children of their own. You have me here and my parents have your son over there. You are good to me, mother, so very good to me that it is impossible to remember the dead. I hope my parents are good to your son, too." I closed my eyes to stop her from reading too much in them. Then I sprang up and said, "I'll go for firewood now."

That was the last time I saw her. I ran all the way to the forest, not knowing whether I would come back with wood or be too angry to collect any. Mother had said that they were going to have a big day for me. Was it not obvious what kind of a big day it would be?

5

A dangerous escape

In the forest I tried to concentrate on collecting wood, but found it impossible to see the dry wood from the rest owing to the tears that were streaming from my eyes. I chose a big log and sat down in an effort to steady myself. I had been sitting there for a long time and was just making up my mind to go back when I heard a familiar voice calling, "Chesebe, I see you are also trying to find wood." It was Chepteek, the one person I wanted to meet more than anyone else in the world.

I stood up and ran to her, "Help me, Chepteek. I want to run away. Help me now, because I am in trouble and cannot stay any longer. Please help me."

Chepteek laughed and said nothing. I told her about the plans being made for me to marry the chief. She warned me of the danger that lay before me. The Tondo law, she said, was to kill any prisoner who tried to escape. She told me that it would be better for me to accept the marriage, and then make careful plans to escape later. She added that once I was married there would be nobody watching over me. She warned me that there were always people watching my movements, and that an attempt to escape might land me right into their net. "All the same, I'm quite willing to help you if you are determined to try."' She looked away from me, then added thoughtfully. "I feel that the number of people I have helped is very small. I wish I could have done better." I assured her that I definitely wished to escape. We kept silent for a long time, I, weighing every word she had said, and she, trying to think out a way of escape. "I'll try it, but come, they will be looking for you now. You have been here for too long. They'll soon be here. Let's be going." She took my hand and pulled me roughly.

"No! Where are we going?" I resisted.

"Come along at once!" she insisted. "You're in trouble and must be helped. I'm the only friend who have to help you now, so you must do everything I tell you."

She dragged me to a pile of wood that she had collected. "Sit down," she ordered in a whisper. I sat down sweating and trembling. She had not said where she intended to take me. She had not even asked me where I would like to go. She threw down the leather straps she used for tying wood together and began to arrange pieces of wood on them.

"May I help?" I asked, shaking.

"No, sit still." She added, "I want you to lie here on the wood. I'm going to tie you up in this bundle and take you home."

"No, please!" I began to protest, but she seized and pushed me down on the pile. Before I could manage to struggle to my feet, she had piled more wood on top of me and was drawing the straps together.

"It hurts!" I cried, but she took no notice of my complaints as she tightened the straps more and more, and then threw her big skin cape over the bundle. I felt I was going to be suffocated. Pieces of wood pricked my skin, and thorns scratched my face but my friend was not concerned about my physical discomforts. She tried to lift the bundle on to her head but found it too heavy, so she rolled it along the ground and put it on a nearby log, then kneeling down on one knee lifted it on to her head. When she had raised herself to her feet she hurried towards her home.

Presently she called in an unsteady voice. "Chesebe, they are coming. Men with clubs and spears are coming. Do not speak! Do not stir."

My heart began to beat hard, the pains in my body were forgotten. I could hear running footsteps which soon stopped, and a voice said, "Have you seen a little girl passing here?"

"How long ago?" Chepteek asked, steadying her voice.

"Just a little while ago," they answered.

"I saw the little Bukusu girl," she said, and my heart almost stopped beating. "Is she the one you are looking for? Chesebe, the little girl who lives with Mutua? I saw her hurrying along the forest path, but when she saw me, she ran back and took the path that leads to the east. She was crying. Are you afraid that something has happened to her?"

They did not answer. They pushed Chepteek aside and ran off to the east to find the lost girl. I whispered my gratitude to her.

She walked unusually fast, breathing hard because of the heavy bundle that she carried. She had been walking for some time when I realized that she was getting tired; her breathing was becoming more difficult. I asked her to put the bundle down and rest. At first, she objected but, after I had begged many times, she set it down and sat on the edge of the path to rest. She had been sitting there for only a few minutes when the searchers reappeared, wet with sweat and very angry.

"Have you seen the ugly little thing again?" one of them asked.

"No, son, I have not seen her. She went the other way. Judging by the way you are running about; she could easily evade you. You should run quickly, and stop from time to time to look through the bush. There are no footmarks here in the mud, so she cannot have come this way. My eye is older than yours, sons, but it would soon see signs of the girl if there were any. You have better eyes. Do you see any footprints along the road?"

They glanced at each other. They had obviously not looked for any. "No, mother," their spokesman said. "We have not looked carefully; we still think she is hiding in the forest somewhere, but we are sending four of our men to watch the boundary. There is only one bridge over the river and we are sure she has not crossed it yet. We shall catch her there, and when we do, we shall drain her blood and quench our thirst with it. She has given us a lot of trouble." He finished and hurried away from us. I listened with interest as the sound of their hurrying feet died away in the distance.

It was clear that they were determined to obstruct all the roads leading out of the forest. "How is Chepteek going to get me across the bridge?" I fought to myself as she struggled again to get her valuable bundle on to her head.

"Chesebe!" she whispered, as she hastened down the path. "Don't be afraid. They'll never set their eyes on you as long as you stay close to me. They are only men. They have no powers of observation. They cannot discover the secret of a woman, a woman like me. They think running is the only way of finding the lost. Let them go," she continued. "I've no sympathy for them. Let them run and sweat blood, but they will not find you."

Sometimes as she swayed from side to side the wood splinters pierced my flesh so much that I wished she had allowed me to walk. "Mother," I called at last. "I want to walk. I want to help you carry the wood. Put me down."

"Stop talking," she whispered. "We're nearing the bridge where they sit to watch." She had not moved forward very far when I heard someone say, "Mother, have you seen any sign of her?"

"The girl? Why, no, I told you that she took the path

along the forest to the east. You seem to be allowing her to get away easily. If that little girl gets out of this country, you will all be captured by the Bukusu tribesmen. She has learned all your secrets. She knows all about your way of life. Other children have taught her how to fight, and how you have managed to conquer so many tribes. We told you to kill that child a long time ago. You looked at her beautiful face and said that she would make a good wife for the chief. We told you to keep her tied up. You looked at her deceitful eyes and said that she would be faithful to her foster-parents. Now you have it!" she mocked. "Don't sit here and look stupid. You cowards! Go and look for the child, out there towards the land of her people! She is probably already there telling them what cowards you really are. You are too afraid to do it! You want to save your own lives! You cowards!" Brandishing, her long stick, she spat at them in pretended fury. "She'll be back again soon with her warriors, and before we know it, we shall all be killed, and whose fault will it be? If none of you will go and find the girl, I'll call the women together, and we shall go to attack the Bukusu in order to bring the child back. I will lead them myself. We shall show you how. You dogs, you trembling chicken-hearted fools!" She pushed her way through the silent company and walked over the bridge proudly. She had won. We were safe.

I looked through an opening in the firewood and saw them. She had abused them in a way that perhaps no Tondo warrior had ever been abused before.

No member of the Tondo tribe would stand such scathing words. I saw them talking together for some time and then they sped off past us. "We shall bring her back," they shouted, as they rushed away. I knew then that there would be trouble in my land, but was happy in the knowledge that a handful of Tondo warriors could do nothing against a band of prepared Bukusu warriors. I knew they would fall as fresh grass before a sharp sword. I knew it, and was sorry for them.

Chepteek took me safely to her home. After she had regained her energy, she told me where she had planned to keep me for several weeks until the Tondo forgot about my escape.

"There is a cave in the side of the mountain," she said. "You'll live in there for a few weeks. Nobody will find you. I'll come in every evening to see you and tell you about the Tondo."

It was very late when she took me to the cave which was very dark, but quite warm. She quietly made my bed and told me to sleep and rest.

For several weeks this was my home. Chepteek came in every evening with enough food for the following day. She sat and talked happily about many things. She told me that she had saved other young people from the Tondo by keeping them in this den. When I asked her about the Tondo warriors who went out to fight, she just laughed. Then one day she told me about them: about their war against the Bukusu, and how only one of them had escaped and run back home. "Without his spear," she finished, laughing. The rest had been killed as they tried to cross the mountain. The chief had called a big meeting at which he announced that the warriors had to be stopped from crossing the boundary because the Bukusu had become very strong since the last war, and that any attempt to attack them would have to be carefully planned.

The chief had promised fifty cows to anybody who would bring him back the girl, either dead or alive. "She has been responsible for the death of my best warriors. If she is alive, she must die a merciless death," he had said.

Chepteek told me many stories. She loved to talk about her youth. She had been a very active girl and had taken delight in fighting other girls. Then one day she told me the whole truth. "Chesebe, I love you very much. I think I will tell you the truth about myself. I am not a Tondo. I was brought into this country as a prisoner of war long before the present warriors were born. I was just a little girl then; much younger than you. I was taught to speak the Tondo language and was changed into a Tondo. I have always wanted to go back to my people but now it is too late. The most I can do is help people like you to escape. The Tondo married me to a man whom I did not like. He had many wives and treated us all like slaves.

"I was very glad when he died at war a long time ago. I refused to marry again. Since that time, I have helped people of our tribe to escape. You will be safe, my girl. I will ask only one thing of you. I want you to be brave enough to lead our people here to come and fight the

Tondo who have now become very weak. They drink a lot, and fight each other so much that they cannot defend themselves against our people. The best time to attack is at the full moon. It is then when they all move away from their watch towers and come home to drink. For one week during this time they drink every night. You know their villages well enough to lead our people to them. Lead them, and make sure that you capture all the villages." She looked at me admiringly. "Chesebe, when you come, remember me."

"I will. If I get a chance to help anyone it will be you, I will help you to escape from this place," I promised.

Time slipped by, and along with it my desire to escape. I was getting so used to life in the cave that did not want to go away. But one day something changed my mind for me. It happened one afternoon, shortly after Chepteek had gone home: I heard the piteous cry of an animal in distress, I listened again carefully. This time I heard the angry snarl of another animal, which I thought might be a lion. I looked out, and as these creatures drew nearer to the cave, I saw that one was a mountain goat of the type common in that area, and it was being chased by a lion. Faster and faster the goat ran but faster still the lion followed. I began to shake with terror as, with bated breath, I watched their approach, and my legs finally failed to hold me up. What if the animal should come into the den? What would happen? It did happen: the goat dived into the cave at a neck-breaking speed, with the lion close behind her. Then propelled by a mighty power,

he jumped on top of the helpless beast. The commotion which followed is hard to tell in words, but there were screams of pain mingled with roars, followed by weak groans, and then the sound of breaking bones. My jaw dropped; my breath stopped. I was petrified. My horror-stricken eyes stared in awful fascination as the lion closed his eyes each time, he brought his teeth together to break the bones. His red eyes, his pointed teeth, his heavy paws, all were terrifying. The groans of the goat had died away; she was dead. While the time dragged by, the hungry lion feasted there in my presence. My fear mounted every minute as he reduced the big goat to small pieces. I felt sure that he would spring at me next, and I closed my eyes waiting for the worst to happen, but it did not. When he had finished his feasting, he dragged the remaining carcass and dropped it on top of me as I lay there half dead. After this he walked to the doorway and settled down to rest.

All this time the lion had obviously thought of nothing but his prey. He had not sensed my presence. He was satiated; but what would stop him from scenting me with the return of hunger? For a longtime the beast lay stretched across the doorway completely blocking it, and making escape impossible. Once or twice I peered in his direction, hoping against hope that he had walked out, but there he was, lying full length across the opening, sound asleep.

I let my mind wander away from the present problems, and thought of the days my brother and I had spent together looking after cattle. I remembered the loving care of my mother and grandmother. I thought of my strong father who had been so good to us, I remembered all this as I laid down my weary head to sleep.

When I woke up it was late evening. The rays of the sinking sun shone red on the beast in the doorway. The animal was no longer asleep. He sat there cleaning his teeth with his long tongue. I looked at his big mouth and smiled into the face of danger. A feeling of pride flooded my heart with the knowledge that I was one of a few human beings who had observed so dangerous an animal at such close quarters. I watched his ribs move up and down as he breathed, and laughed to myself that I was still alive. Nothing worried me now. I wanted to die. I saw no way of escape whatever with the lion sitting there in, the doorway. My heart was pounding so loud in my ears that I feared its beating would be heard.

Then the beast stood up, stretched himself as if to test how he felt, and turned towards the carcass and me. For a long time, he stood there apparently contemplating something, and then he deliberately walked up to me, placed his paw on my bare foot and resumed his chewing of the goat. He took only two or three bites, after which he dragged the carcass out of the cave and walked away. I could not believe my eyes, but there he was pulling his catch along with him.

I waited and after what seemed a very long time, I heard his roar echoing in the mountains. He had gone, leaving me alive and without a scratch.

Exhausted, I lay there thinking. I did not know exactly what to do, but I knew that I had to leave the cave, so I stood up, cleaned my blood-spattered face with my leather skirt and staggered out.

What happened as I made my way to Chepteek's home is not clear, but I remember that on reaching there I stumbled through the doorway, fell down in front of Chepteek and fainted. When I came to myself she was kneeling beside me spraying some water on my face. "I'll be all right" I assured her, fumbling for words. In a trembling voice she asked, "Are you badly hurt, Chesebe?"

"No, I'm not hurt at all. I'm quite all right." "Then what about the blood?"

I closed my eyes while she comforted me and sought to know what had happened. I told her the whole story, from the time I saw the lion chasing the goat to the time I came to her. She listened in amazement, and after I had finished, she went to the door and closed it.

"Chesebe," she said, as she walked back to me. "You're the luckiest person alive. A lion has a very good sense of smell and should have detected your presence. The ones that live here are man-eaters. I fail to understand why you were not attacked." For a long time, we sat talking. She claimed that I had been saved by the spirits of my ancestors so that I might lead my people to conquer the dreaded Tondo.

On the night following that, I received a great surprise.

"Chesebe," Chepteek called in a sleepy voice, "I cannot keep you here tonight. You will have to go. I want you to go away to your people."

"How can I go to my people alone when I don't know the way?" I argued. "You have been so kind to me, grandma; you cannot turn against me now. I can only go away if you allow me to go back to the old chief. I have no other home to go to."

Chepteek stared at me with an expression of mixed pity and indignation. "You will go," she ordered with definite firmness. "You do not know the danger that hangs over your head. Almost every night my hut has been searched with infinite thoroughness because of you. Men all over the country bewail and lament their warriors who died in trying to recapture you. The chief who should have married you will now only accept your head."

She pulled me on to my feet and repeated her order more firmly. "You must go, Chesebe! You'll have to go to your people. I've always told you that they need you, The more I think of the responsibility laid upon you to give your people the information you have, the more I blame myself for having kept you this long."

We stood there in silence; I, with feelings of desolation and despair, and Chepteek, apparently searching in her mind for a kinder way of turning me out of her home.

Outside, the innocent moon was shining brightly, stealing in a beam here and a beam there through the cracked walls and tattered roof of the old house. By the light of these beams I could see her eyes, furious and unrelenting, but with unmistakable kindness deep inside them. I could see for the first time that she had once been a beautiful woman, but her beauty had been erased by the cares of this world.

"I'm not going, Chepteek. If the Tondo must kill me, let them do it here in your house. I'm not going out to them. I'm not leaving the safety of your protection to look for a lonely death. I'd rather die in your arms in this little house than in a Tondo's palace. Please, grandma, let me stay. If I am not killed.

"No, Chesebe." She cut me short. "If you stay here, you'll live only a few days at the most. Others have been killed in this land by trying to hide in people's homes. The Tondo are not fools. They'll find you and kill you. I'd rather see you die in the fields or trying to cross the mountain than be found sitting here."

A mist covered my eyes and my unhappy heart beat faster while my mind raced through the hidden world in search of another refuge from my immediate troubles. The mist gave way to streaming tears and Chepteek's eyes could do no better. In a miserable state of confusion, I fell on her bosom and cried my heart out.

6

The farewell

It was almost morning when she tightened her hold on me and said dreamily, "The cocks will soon crow. You must leave now. I will take you across the river Suswa and show you the way from there. You'll not need to take any food. There's plenty of fruit in the country at this time of the year. Eat it. Our people have a saying that, 'A traveller is a pauper, even though he may be a king.' You may have eaten well while you stayed with Kiprono's family, but now you will eat what you can find. Do not make a fire to cook anything. Eat roots and fruits and leaves; these do not require cooking. Do not go into anybody's home to ask for food or drink. Sleep in hiding during the day and travel during the night. If you meet people, do not ask them the way to such and such a place; behave as if you belonged to the places through which you pass." Then, as if remembering something that she had forgotten, she hastily dragged me towards the doorway and together we stepped out into the cold world under a starry sky.

Cocks were crowing in the scattered neighbouring villages. Soon they would be joined in song by the birds. We walked quietly through the thickets, taking cover under low branches whenever we heard a sound or saw any movement. By the second crowing of the cocks we had reached the river Suswa. Its waters murmured good wishes to us as we stepped from stone to stone in order to cross to the other side. Chepteek drew a palmful of the warm morning water and filled her mouth with it. After we had crossed the river, she sprayed the water from her mouth over my head in a gesture of farewell, saying, 'Go well. Be led by the spirit of our people. Be protected and led by the spirit of your grandfather and the spirit of your father. Let the jaws of wild beasts which you will encounter on your way be locked that they may not harm you. Let their ears be closed that they may not hear your careless steps. Let their eyes be blinded that they may not see you. Let the spirit of provision bring food to your path that you may be filled. May the spirit of goodness cause those who would plan to do you harm to fall into the sea of Walule, and those who would stop you from passing through their country to disappear in the Sea of Sisumo. Go!" she said, almost abstractedly. "Go in peace."

Then, placing a short stick sharpened at both ends in my hand, she continued, "Take this; you may need It. You have learned how the Tondo use this kind of thing. If you need it to protect yourself, use it. Keep calm if you are attacked by an animal. All animals are cowards by nature. If you face a leopard or a lion with a brave determined look, he will not be so likely to attack you. If you become frightened and begin to run away, he will certainly follow you. Be brave. Use the wisdom you have gained from these brave fighters. No Tondo would run away from any living animal. You will make yourself inferior to them by running away." Then, placing her hand on my trembling ones, she said in finality, "Go!"

I walked away silently, afraid to turn my head in case my young heart would urge me to go back.

Yard by yard I walked, striving not to cry and yet unable to control the torrential tears that flooded my eyes and streamed down my cold cheeks. Presently I summed up enough courage to look back, and there was Chepteek still standing with her right hand raised in what seemed to be a gesture of a final farewell. The sight of her increased my longing to fight once more against being sent away. I rushed back and threw myself at her feet, and when I gazed at her in despairing appeal for permission, I saw an expression of triumph in her eyes. What could that wicked twinkle mean?

"Grandma," I pleaded, "let me go back home with you. You know how much I love you. Nothing would make me happier than to live with you for the rest of my life. It is a long time since I came here; I do not know the way home, but I do know that there will be great danger from wild animals, and tremendous difficulties in crossing the mountain from this side. Then there are the unfriendly tribesmen, the Tondo, the Gonyi. I cannot, I dare not go alone. The ..."

"Not alone, Chesebe, not alone." She protested, again with that mysterious twinkle in her eye as she gracefully threw her skin cape over her strong lean body. "I am not asking you to go alone. I would not do it alone myself and it would be evil of me to expect you at your tender age to make the journey all by yourself."

"But that is what you have said." I argued. "You pave dragged me out of your house and sent me on my way to face wild animals and fierce men, all alone. I realize that your life would be endangered if I stay with you for only one more day. Can it be that you see me merely as a roaming foreigner who may bring bad luck to you, or a parasite that would never be of any use to you? Perhaps you are thinking of the old saying: 'A pretending stranger always drives out the owner of the land.' I'm not that kind of person, Grandma. I love you. I want to be your child, or your grandchild. I want to be to you what I'd have been to my parents. Do please allow me to stay."

For the first time, I could see that my pleas had touched her heart-strings and that she was finding it very hard to part with me. I had won half the battle. Clutching her legs as a child does when her mother is moving away, I urged, "Let us go home, Grandma. I belong to you now."

Then the wicked twinkle and look of triumph returned. "No," she replied firmly, "We cannot go back. I'd rather accompany you to your home; it would be safer to do that, but I am not going with you." Then, with a radiant smile of satisfaction she said, "I've arranged for someone else to go all the way with you."

"To go with me, you mean?" I questioned in wonderment. "All the way?"

"Yes, all the way, my child. There is another girl, Jebet by name, who is unknown to you. She's lived in a cave quite close to where you were staying. She came to me two harvests ago, but I've not been able to get her out of the country because of the close watch that has been kept by the people of this tribe. She is a girl of your age, from your own country, and so you will travel together. I told her to wait for you under that huge *Mulemba* tree over there." She pointed out a large *Mulemba* tree a short distance ahead of us. "Go!" she repeated, pulling me on to my feet. "Travel happily together."

I ran off towards the tree, partly afraid that Chepteek was only playing a trick on me, so that she might disappear before I could manage to get back to her, and partly anxious to prove the truth of her statement. On a small boulder under the tree sat the girl of the cave who was to become my companion on this journey. When she heard my tread, she jumped up and began to run away, but on seeing who it was coming towards her, she stopped and eyed me dubiously. "Are you er... Jebet?" I stammered, moving closer to her.

"Yes," she answered, appearing to be ashamed of her nervousness.

"I'm Chesebe — I mean, Nanjala. The Tondo call me Chesebe, but my real name is Nanjala. I'm a Bukusu from Sikulu in the Sirisia valley. Chepteek told me to look for a girl under this tree. Are you the girl?"

"Yes," she answered bashfully. "I'm glad you have found me. My real name is Nekoye. I'm also a Bukusu by tribe, from Malakisi. I was captured by Tondo warriors many years ago when I was only a very small girl. I've grown up with the Tondo people. I can remember very little of my country and my people. I'm glad we can travel together."

Nekoye looked beautiful. I could see her brown skin glistening in the setting moon. The faint smell of fresh cow fat reminded me of the great care that Chepteek had taken of her own skin and that of those who had lived with her. Nekoye's shoulders looked full and fleshy from good feeding. Her thick legs were a clear indication of hardiness. Her short curly hair spread over her head in small uneven heaps, and when she talked, she spoke clearly in such good Tondo that no one would have thought her a foreigner. Instinctively, I took a liking to her, and felt sure that she would make a good companion for the long journey which we had to make.

We set off quietly through the open countryside with mixed feelings. Sorrow, uncertainty and fear began to weigh heavily on our hearts as we strode along together. The wooded country began to close in on us, the path became less defined. With each step we took, our enthusiasm dwindled. Nekoye walked a few yards ahead of me with short quick steps, which made it difficult for me to keep pace with her. Her calf-hide skirt, reaching almost to her ankles, swished through the grass as she hustled along.

After some time had gone by, we noticed the eastern sky change from a light grey to a bright hazel, announcing the approaching sun. "Nekoye," I called, "I think we ought to find a place where we can hide ourselves until night comes again. It will soon be broad daylight and there will be people travelling on this path."

"I'm looking all the time for a suitable tree in which to hide. I know that it's time for us to rest." She continued walking and looking here and there for a tree.

"Look! here is one!" She pointed to a huge *Musemwa* tree on the banks of a small brook. "That seems to be a good tree." We went up to it and found that it was adorned with beautiful ripe fruit; it offered a place to rest our tired bodies as well as food for our hungry stomachs. The branches would provide beds, and the foliage excellent concealment from prying eyes.

We had been up there for only a few moments when the golden rays of the morning sun touched the top of the mountain, revealing giant rocks of all shapes and every description. Soon the birds began to come to the big tree for their morning meal. So, bird and man joined together happily in sharing the succulent fruit.

7

Encounter with a snake

The time that elapsed before we reached the foot of the mountain was filled with pleasant adventure. Nekoye proved to be such a good leader on the journey, and so well informed about the animals and plants of the country that I felt myself to be an ignorant little girl. She seemed to know every tree by name, and every bird and every animal was commonplace to her. She knew almost every edible leaf and root that we came across on the mountainside. She could follow a bee in order to find honey in the way that a dog follows the scent of an animal. She scooped out the honey skilfully from the holes in the ground and the hollows in the trees. It was impossible for me to equal her skill.

On the morning of our third day of travelling, while we were still in high spirits and feeling assured of our safety because of the great distance we had put between us and the Tondo homes, we came upon something most unexpected. As usual, Nekoye was walking ahead of me, her hair covered with the misty dew of the morning. Her skin skirt was also bathed in dew which dripped off as she walked, her upright posture on such a steep incline an indication of her stamina and determination. I was walking behind her with my head lowered in thoughtful meditation when

I suddenly realized that she had stopped and was listening intently with her hand raised in a signal of caution. At first, I could hear nothing, then after some moments of strained listening, I picked out the jubilant voices of warriors coming from up the mountain. The sound drew nearer and nearer. "These are the Tondo raiders. They must be returning from a raid in our country," she said in a whisper. "This is a good sign. We shall follow the trail they have made. Now we shall experience no more difficulty in finding the way."

"We must hide before they reach us," I suggested, trembling with fear.

"Nonsense, Nanjala. If we hide, we shall be spotted and killed or taken back to the Tondo country which will be just as bad as being killed. We also want to learn the news about our country. We cannot run away. We must decide to meet them. I'll speak to them. You should say nothing in case they pick you out as a foreigner. We ought to be able to get through without much trouble."

Nearer and nearer the Tondo marched. The nearer they came the more my courage failed me. "Follow me!" Nekoye ordered, running joyfully as soon as she spotted the first Tondo. She ran up to one of the warriors, jumped high in the air and then, according to custom, grasped the man's wrist and stretched his arm upwards as a sign of great respect. This gesture caused the men to sing much more lustily and dance more vigorously.

After congratulating the warriors on their successful raid, Nekoye told them a pathetic story of how we had lost our animals and were out searching for them. She explained that we lived on the slopes of the mountain and had a large herd of animals that had been captured and brought from a far country. She asked them if they had seen any animals along the way. Not suspecting that they were being deceived, the Tondo expressed their concern for us and promised to keep an eye open for the lost animals. They said they would come back and tell us if they found them. Thus saved, we were left to continue our imaginary search.

When the climb began to be difficult, Nekoye led me along with such understanding that I wondered how I had ever dreamed of making the journey alone. She was brave, very brave, almost too daring for her age. There was nothing on the mountain that seemed to frighten her, or even make her check her speed. She always seemed to be ready with a solution for every situation that arose. She went through the bush fearing nothing. When I asked her if she was ever afraid of wild animals, she only shook her head and said nothing for a long time. Then, as if on second thoughts, she began to rattle off excitedly, "I've encountered most of the animals that a man would be afraid of, and now feel convinced that none of them is really as fierce or even as clever as people think. Take a lion, for example: he does not live up to, his reputation. Face a lion with determination and he will run away. The snake is another example: very few snakes will attack a person unless they are startled. Many other animals are the same. They will never attack just for the sake of attacking."

At the beginning of our journey we travelled at night and rested during the day in order to avoid being detected. As we got farther away from inhabited places, we changed our plan and travelled during the day, using our nights for rest. This plan helped us in more ways than one. We were able to see better during the day, and so avoid sharp stones, boulders and gulleys. These had impeded our progress at night. The most important factor was that we needed to follow the tracks made by the Tondo warriors whom we met on the way. This could be done successfully only by making use of the daylight. It was also easier for us to choose our path better in the daytime.

One mid-afternoon, Nekoye demonstrated to me exactly how brave she was. She was walking only a few paces ahead of me, her hand raised above her shoulders in defiant pride because of her success so far, her strong legs lifting and coming down heavily in the biting cold wind, her broad shoulders swinging rhythmically as they kept time with her legs. Her gait radiated strength and determination. I watched her so closely that I found myself swinging my shoulders in time with hers.

While I was enjoying this steady rhythmic walk, Nekoye stopped as if she had seen a fierce animal. "What is it?" I asked, looking round and expecting to see a lion or leopard, or a pack of wild dogs, but I could see nothing in the vicinity. "What is it Nekoye?"

I pressed, anxious to know what I was missing.

"Shhhhhh!" she hissed, warning me of danger and cautioning me to take care. Then I saw a huge brown snake a few yards in front of her. Its head was raised well above the tall grasses and its fiery tongue waggled quickly in and out of its mouth.

I was petrified, but Nekoye faced the reptile without flickering an eyelid. She held her leather cape shoulder high while she looked at the snake in disdain. Then, as the creature made as if to attack her, she began to defend herself with the dexterity of a trained warrior. Tuk! came the lashing sound on the skin cape as if it were being hit by a whip. I expected to hear Nekoye cry out, but not a sound came except that made by the snake as it repeatedly flung itself at the cape with which Nekoye shielded herself against each attack. Gradually the onslaughts became less violent until they stopped completely and the snake glided away, apparently defeated. Still holding her skin cape, Nekoye followed it. Then it reared itself up and renewed the fight. Again Nekoye defended herself with skill and bravery, never knowing from which side the snake would attack but always deftly covering herself at the right moment. With failing energy, the snake raised its head, its tongue still working, and its tail gently hitting the ground. It seemed not to know what to do next. At this point, Nekoye made one wild leap, jumped on the snake and covered it with her cape.

It coiled and twisted under the cape and lashed out with its tail, but Nekoye held it down while she shouted, "Get me a stone." I obeyed as fast as I could. Holding the snake with one hand, Nekoye crashed down on its head with the stone. "It's finished," she gasped, as she subsided on the ground next to the dead snake. "That was a hard fight," she observed with considerable pride. Then she stood up and threw her cape over the branch of a tree and after some moments of thought she placed the snake with its belly showing to attract the vultures.

When we set out on our journey again, Nekoye talked a little about how different snakes fought, after which we settled down once more to our journey. I was feeling the strain of nervous exhaustion, but Nekoye seemed never to tire. I think I felt it much more than she, or at least showed it much more. From time to time Nekoye had to turn back and give me a helping hand because I was unable to climb a rock, or found difficulty in pulling myself up a slope. Her skill in climbing drew out my admiration for her, and filled me with shame for myself when I found that even very small rocks challenged my courage.

8

The fatal fall

We had been walking for many hours on this particular day without making much progress when we approached a bluff which we would have to climb. It was obviously going to be difficult. "We shall have to avoid that rock face, Nekoye," I said as we pressed on towards it.

"Nonsense, Nanjala. This is only a small row of rocks. We shall climb it without much trouble; just wait and you will see."

The closer we came to the rock face, the more dangerous it looked. Yet to bypass it would have added many weary hours to our journey. Again we were dependent upon the trail that the Tondo warriors had left, so we should have to brave it.

"I do not know how they ever brought their animals over this cliff," I wondered, thinking aloud.

"That is quite easy. The Tondo throw quick bridges across rivers and narrow valleys. Then they destroy the bridges as soon as they have crossed them in order to make it difficult for anyone who may be following. You see that smoke over there? That must be the place where they crossed and where they burned their bridges. We shall have to climb the rock, we certainly cannot make a bridge."

We moved on to the foot of the rock. When I looked at it, I knew at once that it would be impossible for me to scale it. For Nekoye it was a different story. She fastened her cape around her waist and began to climb. She braced her feet in the cracks of the rock with an agility I had never known. Up and up she went, quickly feeling for a crack here and crack there where she could get a foothold. Finally she gathered up all her strength and lifted herself on to the top of the bluff.

All this time, I had been holding my breath as I watched, expecting her to slip and drop back at every step, but it did not happen. On reaching the top, she sat down and looked at her feet with interest.

"Have you hurt yourself?" I called when I saw her examining her feet.

"Not much," she answered, smiling, "but it was very rough going." She stood up and walked along the bluff looking for a better place for me to climb. She did not succeed, so came back and told me that the place she had used was the best. "Come up," she ordered. "Do exactly as I did, and look up. Don't look down. You will be all right. Try it. You'll find it easier than you think. Come!"

"No!" I wailed. "I cannot do it. I'll try to find a better way. I'm quite sure that I'd forget to look up all the time. I'd look down and then fall off."

"Nonsense, Nanjala. You will be all right. You saw how I did it. Use the same method."

Refusing to take her advice, I walked away in the hope of finding a better place to climb. "Come!" she insisted. "You see there is no better place than the one I used."

I continued my search, but did not find a better place. The face of the rock had sharp stones that towered higher, and higher above me as I walked along. "Don't be a coward, Nanjala. Make an attempt to climb." Nekoye ran up the hill and picked a branch from a fallen tree. "Come now. I'll help you with this. Hold on to it and I'll pull you up." She lowered the branch and I grabbed it and held on to it with all my might. "Get ready!" she ordered. "Up!" she commanded with authority. "Up!" she repeated, pulling the branch with all her strength. "Up!" I was now half-way up the rock. Nekoye shouted with delight and infected me with some of her enthusiasm. She was sure that I would complete the climb. Then I glanced down over my shoulder and was horrified to see the distance I had covered. "Up!" Nekoye ordered as she braced herself for a final pull. I made a mighty effort. In the next instant something hit my head, and I knew no more.

I must have lain on the ground for a very long time because when I opened my eyes again, it was late in the afternoon. We had arrived at the foot of the cliff at about the time when dogs steal. Now it seemed to be the time when cattle come home. When I raised my head, a sickening pain shot through it. I lay down trying to recall the happenings of the day and why I was lying there. I was very thirsty, too. Very slowly I looked about me to find out where I was, and as my head cleared, I remembered Nekoye and how she had knelt on the ledge holding the branch, encouraging me to make a supreme effort to reach the top. Where was Nekoye now? Why was she not with me? Had she scrambled down the rock face and tried to carry me to the top and failed? Had she gone for help? Had she gone away altogether and left me in this lonely place? Over and over again these questions raced through my mind.

I sat up and stretched out first one arm and then the other; all was well. Next, I tested my legs in the same way, and finding that my limbs were whole I stood up and was thankful that I was able to walk. With a lump in my throat, I thought of Nekoye. Could it be that she had deserted me in such a difficult place? What should I do? I would never be able to climb that rock by myself. Where could I go? Why had Nekoye behaved in such a way?

In a very troubled state of mind, I was searching for the Tondo trail when I heard a low groan from nearby. I quickly went to the place from where it came, and there Nekoye lay in a pool of blood. She was in great pain. I knelt down beside her and in an anxious voice asked what had happened.

"Nothing much," she answered, barely managing a smile. When she saw the worried look on my face, she tried to stand to prove that she was well. She could not manage it. She fell back on her side and groaned again in pain.

"Nekoye, what happened?"

She looked up at me but did not answer. She tried a second time to get up, but without success. Her face was drawn with pain. With my help, she managed to sit up. I had not yet found where the blood was coming from.

"Are you hurt?" I asked with a note of grave concern in my voice.

"I am hurt, but I don't think it's very serious," she said with difficulty. "It's here." She tried to stretch out her leg to show me, but it remained limp. Then I saw: her thigh bone was protruding through the skin. "Here!" she touched it.

"Good heavens!" I exclaimed to myself when I realized the seriousness of her wound.

A dark cloud of fear swept over me as she fell on her back in pain with her eyes closed. "Nekoye!" I cried anxiously. There was no immediate answer. She was breathing heavily feeling very weak from loss of blood. Something had to be done immediately or else Nekoye would probably die. As fast as I could, I gathered some tall grasses, plaited them and gently bound up her wound taking great care not to cause her more pain. She lay there in a heap, breathing heavily.

The sun was now setting. The biting cold became more than we could bear. I attempted to carry Nekoye to a shelter under a rock which I hoped would protect us from the wind, but she seemed as heavy as the rock that had broken her thigh. I managed to drag her along the ground, stopping every few minutes to give myself a rest to see how she was feeling. I was afraid her strength would give out and that she would collapse at any time. After a long, slow struggle, we reached the shelter. Nekoye had been wonderful. In spite of her extreme weakness she had asked to be allowed to try to walk. Knowing she could not do it, I had ignored her request.

With every passing moment, Nekoye grew weaker and more uncomfortable. Her leg was now swollen from the thigh to the foot. She could neither lie down, nor sit up properly. I let her lean on me in a sitting-lying position all that night and through the days and nights that followed, except when I was away collecting berries or drawing water.

I did not feel hungry at all. I felt so angry with myself all the time that I could not eat. Nekoye never complained. She lay down there smiling through her pain, encouraging me every time she saw despair in my face.

"It'll be all right," she would say smiling. "It's not too bad. I have gone through worse pains than these. Don't worry, Nanjala, it will be all right."

I spent much time trying to comfort Nekoye when I was not looking for food. On the morning of our third day in the cave, she urged me to try and find some help for both of us. She said that her leg was getting worse and that it was no longer necessary for us to remain in hiding.

"Where can I get help?" I asked, frightened at the thought of going back to the Tondo alone.

"Go back to Chepteek. Go back to the Tondo and ask for help. Let them give you men to carry me out of here and heal my wound. I am sure you realize that the air is getting colder and colder each day and soon it will be impossible for us to go away from here. You must leave at once."

"I'll have to find some food for you before I go. I may be away for several days."

"Then don't sit there thinking about it. Every moment counts now. Go and do something."

I went out to look for food. I was terribly frightened when I examined the consequences of this accident. Behind me were the Tondo warriors who had orders to kill me; ahead of me the great forbidding Masaba Mountain, and beside me a dying companion. Nekoye had looked strange to me that morning. The confident smile on her face had disappeared. Her bright eyes had become dull and covered with a cloudy mist.

I collected as much food as I could carry and walked back to the shelter with it. Nekoye was asleep and I did not want to disturb her. I was about to go and fetch water before leaving when she stirred and called faintly, "Nanjala, water please." Between her irregular breathing she mumbled, "Some water please. It's hot here." I knew it was not hot. In fact the morning had had a very unfriendly chill. I went over to the stream and drew some water, carrying it in my cape. I knelt beside her and helped her to drink from the cape. She gulped the water down, then fell back to sleep. I was just beginning to leave again when she called me a second time. "Nanjala." This time her voice was fading.

"Come and listen to me." I moved quickly to her side.

"I don't think your going out to seek help for me will be of use. It will be very difficult for you to get back to Chepteek, and who knows what you will find when you finally get there. Stay with me to the end. I'm dying. We cannot travel together any longer. Our journey together must end here. I'm sorry that you will be left alone." She closed her eyes and seemed to have fallen asleep. Then she opened them again and asked, "Are you listening, Nanjala?"

"Yes, I'm listening," I said, greatly ashamed and distressed at my inability to help. My heart yearned to find a way to help her. I longed to heal her, and yet something inside me said that she would die before anything could be done. I knew she was telling the truth. She was dying. At this thought a lump rose in my throat, and once again tears of sorrow and loneliness rolled down my face.

"Nanjala," she went on, "I'm dying. It has been so good to be with you during the last few days. I had hoped that we would get back to our people together and lead the army to defeat the Tondo, but I have to join my ancestors in the far-off land. They are calling for me. They need me there. I can see the beautiful land to which no man knows the way unless led by the spirit of the dead. Do not give up. Have courage. Go ahead until you cross the great mountain which has killed me. Be careful, but when faced by animals show courage. Courage will be your only protection. From the stories that we have heard, we know that there are many fierce animals on the other side of the moutain; but you have learned how to fight animals. Do not run away."

As I sat there listening with my heart pounding to bursting point with sorrow and anger, Nekoye fumbled at her waist belt and pulled out a small leather bag covered with sea-shells. Inside, there was a tiny talisman which she claimed had helped her all her life. "Take this. It will help you on your way. When you get home, look out for my people and give it to them. They will recognize it. Our clan is the Baliuli of Malikisi. Look for them. My father was Sabwami of the family of Wachana. There are many people who would know my people. Give them this and tell them that I had hoped to live to see them again, but I've been called to join the others yonder. Let them not grieve a second time for me. They grieved before. Yes, when the Tondo took me." Her voice became weaker. I saw that her eyes were clouding over and that she was finding it difficult to open her mouth to speak. "Yes, the Tondo who took me away. Tell them that I lived well with them and have died a brave death." She was quiet for some time. Then livening up again, she said, 'Nanjala, are you there?" She grasped my hand and tried to sit up, but weakness overwhelmed her and she fell back. I noticed that her grip on my arm tightened for a while; then suddenly slackened. She stiffened and opened her eyes. "Nanjala!" she whispered finally. "Nanjala!" Then with a sigh she collapsed and relaxed into her final sleep.

The hours that followed her death were filled with so much desolation that I did not know what to do.

Here was Nekoye, dead. The girl who knew so much about travelling in this difficult country, and who would have led me easily all the way home. Dead because of my miserable self-pity and lack of courage. Now I would have to face the ordeal of traversing the mountain alone, or go back to the Tondo. Neither of these prospects offered any solace.

For a long time I sat beside Nekoye's body, crying and holding her stiff cold hand, wishing every moment that she could come back to life.

It was late in the afternoon. The shadows of the trees were growing longer. Any hope of seeing Nekoye return to life had faded away. In despair, I crawled out of the shelter and went in search of another place in which to rest. When I finally flung myself down to rest my sorrow was almost unbearable; but in spite of this, I made up my mind to continue the journey up the mountain.

"Come what may," I told myself with feminine pride, "I will show the world that I am a Bukusu of the clan of Bamuyonga. I will shake off my fear." Comforted a little I went out and began to prepare to bury Nekoye's body so that it would not be desecrated by hyenas during the night.

The task was long and tiring: I collected stones and piled them one on top of another to block up the entrance to the cave so that animals could not enter; then I carried fallen branches of trees and placed them in front of the stones. There was nothing more that I could do. Sadly I made my way back to my new shelter, exhausted and sleepy.

9

A fight with a lion

The next day I set out on my lonely journey. The climb was torture, every bit as difficult as it had been on the first occasion, and this time I had to depend upon my own skill and wit. After more than one desperate attempt, I reached the top of the bluff, bruised and bleeding from cuts and scratches; but I had done it! In weary elation, I rested there until my energy revived. I found nothing to eat until I reached the forest belt where giant cedar trees towered above me in majestic splendour. Here the colobus, the chimpanzee and the blue monkey created a happy chattering atmosphere. Here also I came upon the carcass of a mountain goat left over from a recent kill. There was no fire to cook the meat, but it was still fresh and succulent, and to my thirsty tongue it tasted sweet.

Day after day I travelled, covering only a short distance in many hours. With every step I took up the mountain side, the air became colder and more unfriendly. This, coupled with the misery of having lost Nekoye, made life harsh. The leather cape which had served me so well on the lower slopes of the mountain and during most of the time I had stayed with the Tondo, now seemed to succeed only in collecting beads of frozen water. My condition was made worse by the gnawing hunger that accompanied me all the time.

The slopes of the mountain were covered with more bamboo trees than I had ever seen. Mile after mile I pressed through the thickly interwoven mountain growth, barren of any fruit, guided only by the trail left behind by the Tondo raiders.

One bright afternoon, after a long lonely journey, I followed a track that skirted a hill. There before my gaze stretched the land I had so much longed to see — my own country — opening before me in a panorama of magnificent African beauty. I was deeply moved and felt great relief that the danger from the Tondo was now over, having been left behind with each dragging step I had made up this mountain. The beautiful scenery and sense of freedom increased my hope and determination to press on towards my goal. No amount of hunger would make me despair now. No physical obstacles would stop me from reaching my people. Spurred by this renewed inspiration, I hurried on down the mountain, not knowing what tests of endurance lay ahead of me.

When I reached the thick bamboo forest again, I noticed fresh elephant dung and the trail that the elephants had made, but as nothing could pow cloud the vision that carried me down the mountain, the spoor did not strike me as being a sign of danger at all.

I passed through the bamboo forest and was just cresting a small hill when I came upon a whole herd of elephants: great big elephants and small baby

ones, fathers, mothers and children, all mixed up in a trumpeting herd. I was terrified, and crept away in fear.

The next moment, I heard a blood-curdling roar behind me. I was being followed by a lion. I swung round to face the animal, and his hair-raising roar seemed to draw me towards him. I had stepped forward with a lunging movement in the form of an attack. This surprised him, and he turned away and started down the hill. Then, as if on second thoughts, he came back and faced me. He held me in his gaze for a moment or two, appearing to examine the double pointed stick held in my trembling hand — my only weapon.

"Come!" I shouted at him in defiance. "Come and meet the bravest Bukusu warrior face to face. Come!" I shouted in desperation. The animal continued his close scrutiny of me, at the same time sweeping his long tongue over his saw-like teeth. I could see his blood-shot eyes steadily narrowing in concentration.

Then suddenly he sprang at me with his mouth wide open.

With Chepteek's words ringing in my ears, I gathered courage, poised my sharpened stick, rushed forward and thrust it into the beast's gaping mouth. As his teeth closed over it, the stick fixed itself between his jaws. The excruciating pain caused him to fall back on his haunches in a confused state of anger and fright while blood spilled from his nose and mouth. With renewed fury, stimulated by the pain from the wound he had received, he sprang at me again knocking me down on my back several paces in front of him. But, because the stick was now so well embedded in his jaws he could do no more than use his paws. Before he had time to step on me, I managed to scramble to my feet and put all my remaining energy into running away. I saw a *Mukhonge* tree with a low lying limb and desperately leapt up to its comparative safety. Breathless, and weak from fright, I sat in the tree and looked to see if the beast was chasing after me. With great relief I saw him still at the scene of our struggle, trying unsuccessfully to push the stick out of his bleeding jaws. Like an escaping monkey, I sprang from one branch to another until I reached the top of the tree. From this safe place I watched him for a long time until he disappeared between some bushes.

When I looked in the direction of the elephants I found that they too had gone away. Hunger and thirst prevented me from sleeping, but I dared not leave the tree until the following day when I hoped to be able to continue on my homeward way in safety.

10

Home at last

At daybreak I started down the mountain, taking extreme care not to be surprised by any more man-eaters. Through fields of ripening millet, and over rolling hills covered with *Minyali* and *Milemba* trees I travelled, carried along more by the burning desire to get home to see my people than by my tired feet.

At about the time when the women come home from their fields, I crossed the Kuywa river at *Lifuvukho lia Sawenja*, a well known ford, and entered the familiar Sirisia valley. Memories of the past flooded my mind as I trod the eroded ground that Kakai and I had traversed on many occasions when we led our animals to drink at the river and to lick the natural rock salts on its gullied banks.

When I reached the place where I had seen the Tondo spy, about seven years before, the same fear filled my being as I saw the Tondo phantom gazing at me from behind that same rock. Scared by my vivid imagination I ran away as I had run those seven years before; but now there was no Kakai to chase after me and no animals to follow us. After I had crossed the Kikuni brook, I stopped and laughed at my childish fear. "You are now a big girl," I reflected to myself. "Why are you running away from nothing? After all, you have faced many dangers much greater than a non-existent Tondo warrior," I mused out loud.

Still anxious to get to my village, I resumed the pace I had adopted when coming down the mountain. As the animals were gathering in the shadows to chew the cud, I reached the place where I was sure our village had once stood. The village was no longer there. Untended tall grass, enriched by cow dung, revealed the site of the cattle enclosures. The singing of the birds in the neglected bushes reminded me of much more than I wished to remember. There were no houses to be seen in any direction. The place was a sorry sight of vanished beauty. Human activities that had given the place the name of the best village in Bukusuland, had been replaced by the natural growth of creepers and wild marigolds. For a long time I stood there waiting for life to spring up behind the bushes, but knowing full well that no life would really appear.

Then, as if driven by a supernatural power, and not knowing really where to go, I stalled off to the eastern side of the deserted ruins. I had been walking for about the time it usually took mother to go from our house to the river and back, when I saw a village on a hill with many houses scattered about on its broad shoulders. "Run!" I ordered myself, as I sped up the hill. Within a very short time I was standing in front of the first house. It was a round hut surrounded by a well-kept hedge. In front of the house I saw a young man of about my age sitting crosslegged, weaving a reed basket. His features seemed familiar, so I stopped in order to study him more carefully. Could it possibly be...? it must be. Yes, it was! It was my brother Kakai! In uncontrollable excitement, I shouted, "Kakai!" I hoped that he would recognize me and rush out to meet me, but he did nothing more than look up, apparently startled by the unfamiliar voice.

"Can ... can... can you guess who I am?" I asked in a faltering way, feeling for the right words with which to introduce myself.

Kakai jumped to his feet and eyed me suspiciously. "How can I guess who you are? I have never seen you before; but I am interested to know who you are."

"Well, I thought you could guess, Kakai. I am your sister, Nanjala." New he was on the alert and scrutinized me more carefully.

"Who says so?" he asked in utter disbelief.

"I do — and I've come," I answered, rather disappointed at his seemingly rude manner of welcoming me.

"Liar!" he shouted pointing his angry finger at me. "You are the poorest imposter I have ever known. You think by learning Bukusu so well you can come and throw dust in our eyes. I lived with Nanjala in one home, shared one bed-roll, spent time in the fields with her every day; gathered the grasshoppers with her for our meals for years. Nanjala was my sister and I knew her so ..."

"If you knew Nanjala so well, then why can you not see that I am she, your sister?" I cut him short.

"Liar! Where are those beautiful teeth, your beautiful ears, your well-formed neck? Where are they, you liar?" With that he rushed into the house to give the news, and I dashed in after him, eager to present myself to anybody who might be willing to listen to me. In the middle of the room stood a woman — my mother — startled by the unexpected commotion.

"What's all this, Kakai?" Mother asked, eyeing me critically.

"This!" Kakai panted pointed at me. "This ugly imposter wants to present herself as our dead girl Nanjala."

"What?" Mother shouted, "Nanjala? Never!"

"Mother, believe me. Please give me a chance to explain. Listen to me," I pleaded.

"No chances, Mother. This is a Tondo spy. Be careful about her. It has happened before, so it can happen again," Kakai warned. "I will have to call someone else to listen to these lies."

"No, Kakai, please don't do that. Listen to me. I am your sister. I was taken by the Tondo warriors when they killed father and many other people in our village over on the other side of the hill, about seven harvests ago. I've lived with the Tondo all these years."

"Mother, I must call someone else," Kakai said, trying to hurry past me.

"No, Kakai listen to me. I'm your sister. I *am* Nanjala. You cannot call in anyone else," I said, indignantly blocking his way. "These markings which

you see on me are only the evil work of the Tondo. I'm Nanjala, a Mumuyonga of the house of Mukhonyi, my grandfather being Mangula and grandmother Mbakhila of the family of Lutukayi, a Tolometi. You, Mother, come from the family of Ngoya of the clan of Bakunga. What other proof do you desire of me?"

"What proof have you given us?" Kakai asked, still anxious to leave the room.

"Listen, Kakai," Mother said. "We shall see." She took me by the shoulders and turned me round, all the time examining my features carefully.

"Mother, be careful about this imposter. She has nothing to prove that she is really Nanjala. Seven harvests are not enough to make a girl look so different. Be careful about what you accept. I know we have an old saying: 'A man who has once been bitten by a snake starts even if he sees a dead palm leaf,' but we have suffered before, and do not want to invite any more troubles. Turn this liar out."

"Be quiet Kakai, we shall soon have the proof we need," she said, still surveying me, her eyes sparkling with interest, although her hands shook. "Could it be? Kakai, could it be? Could it be my daughter Nanjala!" she said uncovering my shoulders. "Kakai!" she shouted in a shaking voice of final acceptance. "Look! Look at this!" she said, pointing to a broad scar on my back where a cow gored me when I was only a little girl. "Look Kakai! It is true. Nanjala!" She seized me and caught me in a lost-child-come-home embrace. For a long time, we stood there in each other's arms, completely overwhelmed by this unexpected reunion.

Thud, thud, thud, was all I could hear as my mother's heart pounded almost to bursting point with joy. Warm tears from her loving eyes ran down my forehead and mingled with my own tears.

When we disengaged from this warm embrace, we found ourselves unable to talk. Silence was the best expression of the deep feelings that filled our hearts. Kakai stood there with his mouth wide open, still struggling with his disbelief.

At last, here I was, at home. For me, it was the end of a terrible adventure that had lasted a long time. For my loved ones, it was like a dream come true.

www.ingramcontent.com/pod-product-compliance
Lightning Source LLC
LaVergne TN
LVHW092056060526
838201LV00047B/1422